ROTTEN RALPH

Written by JACK GANTOS

Illustrated by NICOLE RUBEL

HOUGHTON MIFFLIN COMPANY BOSTON

To Carew

The character of Rotten Ralph was originally created by
Jack Gantos and Nicole Rubel.

ISBN: 0-395-24276-2 REINFORCED EDITION
ISBN: 0-395-29202-6 SANDPIPER PAPERBOUND EDITION
MANUFACTURED IN CHINA

LEO 50 49 48 47 46
4500816760

Library of Congress Cataloging in Publication Data

Gantos, John B
   Rotten Ralph.

   SUMMARY: Ralph, a very, very, nasty cat, finally
sees the error of his ways--or does he?
   [1. Cats--Fiction. 2. Behavior--Fiction]
I. Rubel, Leslie. II. Title.
PZ7.G15334Ro   [E]   75-34101
ISBN 0-395-24276-2

Ralph is Sarah's rotten cat,

but Sarah loves him anyway.

When Sarah practices ballet
Ralph makes fun of her.

One afternoon when Sarah was swinging,
Rotten Ralph sawed off the branch.

The very next day Ralph ruined
Sarah's party. He had taken a bite
out of every one of her cookies.
"Sometimes you are very hard to
love, Ralph," said Sarah.

One day Sarah's father came home
early from work. He caught Ralph
sitting in his favorite chair. Ralph
was wearing Father's slippers and blowing
soap bubbles through his best pipe.
"You are worse than rotten, Ralph,"
said Father.
"I wish you wouldn't upset Father,"
Sarah said.

The next evening Ralph smashed his
bicycle into the dining room table.
Father became very angry.
"You better straighten up, Ralph,"
he said.
"You are a very difficult cat,
Ralph," said Sarah.

After dinner Ralph was still hungry.
He chased Mother's favorite birds. She
was very unhappy with Ralph's behavior.

One evening the whole family went to
the circus. Everyone was having a
great time but Ralph. A dog was barking
in his ear.

"Be quiet!" said Ralph.

But the dog didn't stop. He kept barking
and stomping his paws on the seat.

So Rotten Ralph tied some balloons
to the dog's collar. The dog
floated up over the lion's cage.
"My dog!" shouted the owner.
But not even the man on stilts could
reach him.

Then Ralph saw the trapeze.

He swung and knocked over the

tightrope walkers.

Next he jumped on a showhorse.
He pushed the rider off and frightened
the elephants.

"Rotten Ralph has gone too far this time!"
bellowed Father. "We are leaving him
here! A circus is just where he belongs."
And they left him behind.

When the circus closed that night
the manager made Ralph sweep up all
the popcorn.

Then he had to water the camels.

After that he had to carry the barbells for the strongman.

The next day Rotten Ralph did not
want to work. He refused to be the
target for the knife thrower.
So the circus tough men threw
him in a cage. "Everybody has
to work around here, buster!" the
tough guys said, and they locked
the door.

The monkeys laughed and threw
banana peels at Ralph. The elephants
shot peanut shells at him and
squirted water on him.

A week later Ralph had grown very
thin. He had only been fed stale popcorn
and rotten candied apples.
That night he decided to escape.
Nobody heard him as he slipped between
the bars.

Ralph ran from the circus and
found a place to sleep in an alley.
During the night he was awakened by
gangs of mean and noisy cats. The rest
of the night he hid in a trash heap.
He didn't dare make a sound even though
mice were nibbling on his toes.

In the morning he was cold and sick.

He had caught an alley fever

from sleeping in the trash heap.

"I'm lonely," he thought, and he

began to cry.

He was sitting on a trash can when
Sarah found him.
"Oh, Ralph, I still do love you,"
she said. She was so happy she hugged
him and gave him a kiss on his cold
nose.

On the way home she told him she had
been looking for him everywhere. She
asked him where he had been and what he
had been doing.

Even Sarah's mother and father were
happy to see Ralph again.

"We have missed you, Ralph," they said.

Ralph kept thinking about his soft
bed and warm milk. He also thought about
how nice it was to have a good friend
like Sarah.

Ralph decided never to be rotten again . . .

except for sometimes when Mother
cooked lobster for dinner.